José

AND

El Perro

To Mya, Oliver, and Brady, my four-legged baby—SR

To all the dogs I've loved before—SL

To Francisco José and José Carlos. I couldn't have done this without their support. And to our beloved perros Nube, Mochi, and especially Kumo—GF

PENGUIN WORKSHOP
An imprint of Penguin Random House LLC, New York

First published simultaneously in paperback and hardcover in the
United States of America by Penguin Workshop, an imprint of
Penguin Random House LLC, New York, 2023

Visit us online at penguinrandomhouse.com.

Library of Congress Cataloging-in-Publication Data is available.

Manufactured in China

ISBN 9780593521168 (pbk)   10 9 8 7 6 5 4 3 2 1 TOPL

Design by Jamie Alloy

José
AND
El Perro

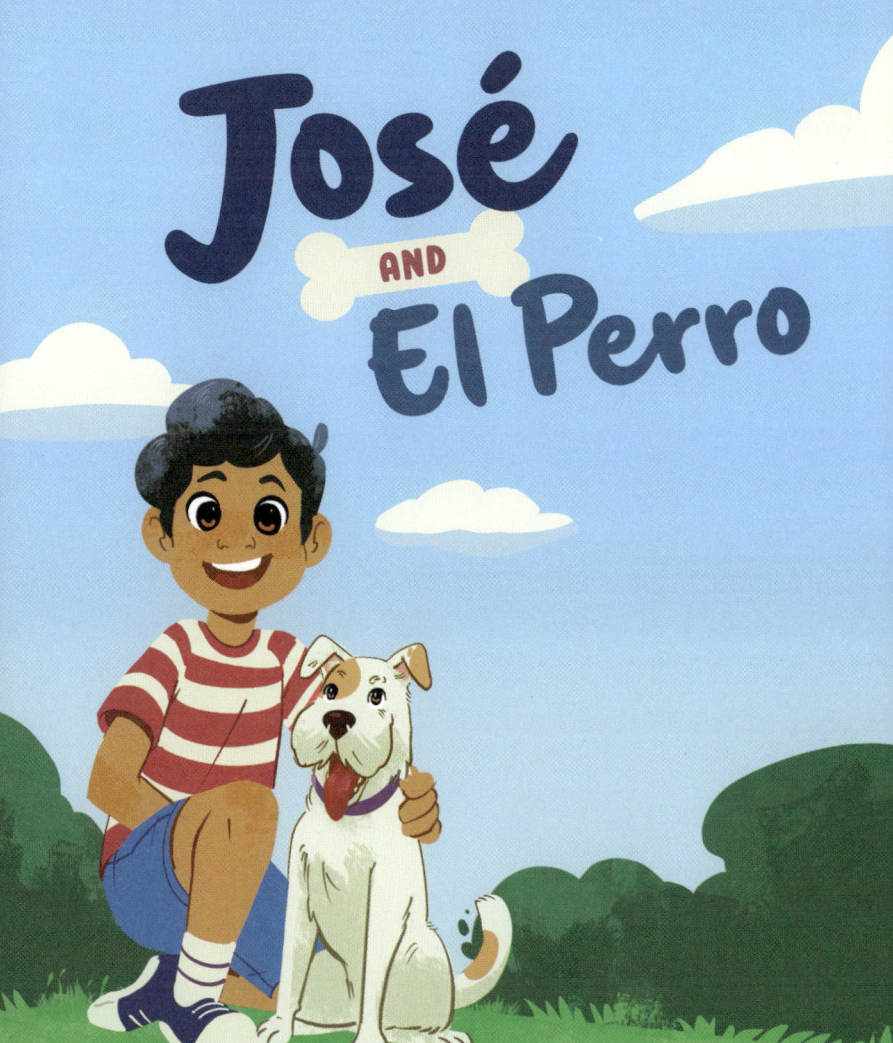

BY **Susan Rose** AND **Silvia López**
ILLUSTRATED BY **Gloria Félix**

PENGUIN WORKSHOP

Chapter 1
The Animal Shelter

José loved his family—Papi, Mami, and little sister Sofi.

But something was missing.

José dreamed of having a dog.

"When can we get un perro?" he asked every day.

One morning, Papi said, "Hoy vamos. We go today."

At the animal shelter, Mami said,
"Time to choose, José."

José looked and looked.

There were perros blancos,
whiter than snow.

Black dogs, like the sky at night.

And all colors in between.

There were perros grandes,
almost as big as José!

Perros pequeños,
as small as Sofi's bear, Fufú.

And all sizes in between.

So many dogs! ¡Muchos perros!

Then José saw a white dog with brown spots.

He liked his colors: blanco con manchas marrones.

He liked his in-between size.

No muy grande. No muy pequeño.

When José came close, el perro gave him . . . una sonrisa!

José smiled back.

A perfect dog. Un perro perfecto.

"I want this one!" José said. "¡Yo quiero este!"

Chapter 2
A Perfect Name

José was excited to see what el perro could do.

"¡Siéntate!" he told the dog.

El perro did **not** sit.

"¡Échate!" José said.

El perro did **not** lie down.

"Maybe if you had a name, you would know what to do," José said.

He wanted to give him a perfect name.

What would be un nombre perfecto?

"How about Manchas?" Mami said.
"He has a lot of spots."

José stared at the dog. El perro stared back. He smiled and smiled.

This is a happy dog, José thought.
Un perro feliz.

That was it!

"I will call you Feliz!" José told him.

Feliz was un nombre perfecto for a happy dog.

Now that Feliz had the perfect name,
José was ready to try again.

"¡Siéntate, Feliz!" he said.

Feliz tilted his head.

First to one side.

Then to the other.

He looked confused.

"¡Feliz, siéntate!" José said again.

"¡Échate, Feliz!"

Nothing. Nada.

José tried over and over.

He even tried showing Feliz.

"Siéntate . . . ," José said. "Like this . . ."

Feliz wagged his tail.

"¡Échate así, Feliz . . . !"
Feliz licked José's face.

José giggled. Feliz was happy.
He was perfect.

But it looked as if he did not know
any commands.

José sat on the ground next to Feliz.

"¿Qué hacer . . . ?" he said. What to do?

Chapter 3
Cookies!

José heard Mami and Papi in the kitchen.
It was Sofi's snack time.

"¿Quieres galletas? Do you want cookies,
Sofi?" asked Mami.

Sofi clapped. "¡Sí, sí, galletas, Mami!
Cookies, cookies, cookies!"

Next to José, Feliz gave a little bark.

His ears perked up.

His tail wagged wildly.

"¿Qué pasa, Feliz?" José asked.
"What's wrong?"

Feliz took off for la cocina.
He slid to a stop by Sofi's silla.

Everyone looked surprised.

José had an idea.

He opened the jar marked "doggie treats."

He found a dog cookie. It was shaped like un hueso.

"Do you want a cookie?" José asked Feliz.
Feliz jumped up and down.
José smiled.

Time to try out
his idea.

"Sit!" José said.
Feliz gave a big bark.
And sat!

José took out another cookie.

"Lie down!"

Feliz did as he was told.

José laughed and laughed.

He hugged Feliz around el cuello.

He kissed him en la cabeza.

He danced with Feliz around the kitchen.

His perfect, happy white-and-brown perro knew commands!

He just did not know Spanish!

Chapter 4
¡Español!

At José's house, everyone spoke English.

Y español.

José couldn't wait to teach Feliz some Spanish words.

He told Mami and Papi what he was going to do.

"Buena idea," Papi said. Mami agreed.

"¡Vamos afuera, Feliz!" José said,
running outside.

He showed Feliz una galleta.

"¡Siéntate!" he said. "Sit!"
Feliz sat, gobbled la galleta, and smiled.

"Good boy! ¡Buen perro!" José said.

José did this again and again.

Feliz got it right again and again.
Perfecto each time.

Then José said, "Let us try something new.
Algo nuevo."

He showed Feliz a cookie.

"¡Siéntate!" he said. But this time, he did not say "sit" in English.

He said the word only en español.

Feliz looked puzzled.

For a few moments, he looked from José to la galleta and back to José.

"¡Siéntate, Feliz!" José said again.

He held his breath. His heart raced. Would Feliz know what to do?

Then, Feliz gave a little bark.

And sat!

José let out a whoop.

"Yes! ¡Eres un perro inteligente!
You are a smart dog!"

He gave Feliz the cookie.
And a great big hug, too!

Every day after school,
José and Feliz raced to el patio.

Feliz learned fast.

¡Échate!

In no time, he knew that
"échate" meant "lie down."

¡Trae!

He fetched la bola when
José said, "¡Trae!"

He came running when José said, "¡Ven!"

If Sofi was sleeping, José told him,
"Shhh, silencio . . ."
Feliz did not make a sound.

One night, Feliz lay down by José.

José petted su perro perfecto.

"I will teach you more words tomorrow," he whispered. "Te quiero mucho, Feliz . . . I love you lots."

Feliz did not need to learn those words. He knew what José meant.

He just closed his eyes. And smiled.

List of Spanish Words and Phrases

El perro: The dog

Un perro: A dog

Hoy vamos: We go today

Perros blancos: White dogs

Perros grandes: Big dogs

Perros pequeños: Small dogs

¡Muchos perros!: So many dogs!

Blanco con manchas marrones: White with brown spots

No muy grande: Not too big

No muy pequeño: Not too small

Una sonrisa: A smile

Un perro perfecto: A perfect dog

¡Yo quiero este!: I want this one!

¡Siéntate!: Sit!

¡Échate!: Lie down!

Un nombre perfecto: A perfect name

Manchas: Spots

Un perro feliz: A happy dog

Nada: Nothing

Asi: Like this

¿Qué hacer?: What to do?

¿Quieres galletas?: Do you want cookies?

Si: Yes

¿Qué pasa?: What's wrong?/What's going on?

La cocina: The kitchen

Silla: Chair

Un hueso: A bone

El cuello: The neck

En la cabeza: On the head

Y español: And Spanish

Buena idea: Good idea

¡Vamos afuera!: Let's go outside!

¡Buen perro!: Good dog!

Algo nuevo: Something new

¡Eres un perro inteligente!: You are a smart dog!

El patio: The backyard

La bola: The ball

¡Trae!: Fetch!

¡Ven!: Come!

Silencio: Quiet

Te quiero mucho: I love you lots

José y Feliz